The Nature Club
Making a Splash

Text copyright © 2019 by Rachel Mazur
Cover illustrations copyright © 2019 by Elettra Cudignotto
Inside illustrations copyright © 2019 by Rachelle Dyer
Edited by Emma Irving and Julie Mazur Tribe

A portion of the proceeds from the sale of this book will benefit frog conservation.

Library of Congress Cataloging-in-Publication Data is available upon request.
ISBN 978-1-7329156-3-3 (paperback)
ISBN 978-1-7329156-8-8 (ebook)

First edition 2019

10 9 8 7 6 5 4 3 2 1

Wild Bear Press operates on the simple premise that nature-based stories connect children with the natural world and inspire them to protect it.

Visit us on the Web! www.natureclubbooks.com

The Nature Club
Making a Splash

Rachel Mazur

WILD BEAR
PRESS

For Max, whose hugs fill my heart and
whose laugh makes me happy

1

Zack stood below an old willow tree in the backyard and stared at a hole high on the trunk. He had seen a woodpecker carry food to the hole enough times to know she had a nest in there. But to see the nest, he needed to peer into the hole, and to peer into the hole, he needed to climb the tree, and to climb the tree, he needed to hoist himself up onto the lowest branch—but the lowest branch was way above his head. He tried taking a running jump to reach it, but it was just too high.

Determined to see the nest, he went to the shed to get a ladder. The only one he could find was the old wooden one his mom had warned him not to use. He couldn't think of any other way to get high enough to peer into the hole, so he dragged the ladder over to the tree and leaned it against the trunk. Zack climbed up to the fourth rung and then stopped—the wood on the fifth rung was starting to split.

Zack tried to peer into the hole from where he stood, but he was too low. He even got up on his toes, but he was still too low. Slowly and carefully, he set his right foot onto the fifth rung and tested it—it felt stable. He put his weight on it and lifted his other foot up toward the lowest branch when . . . *craaack*! The rung broke and Zack crashed to the ground.

He yelled out as he fell, but when he hit the ground, the air was knocked out of him, and he lay quiet. At first, he wondered if he was still alive, but then he felt a sharp pain coming from his left arm. Yup. He was alive. He lifted his head to look at his arm and saw it was bent at an odd angle between his wrist and elbow. Feeling a mix of pain, nausea, and panic, he yelled, "IZZY!" before laying his head back down.

Izzy, who was sitting on the back porch reading, heard a crash, followed by her little brother yelling for help. She threw down her book and ran toward Zack's voice, finding him at the base of the old willow tree. In stark contrast to his bright-red hair, Zack's face looked pale and afraid.

"I think it's broken," Zack said in a daze.

"It sure is," Izzy agreed, looking at the broken ladder on the ground next to him.

"No, Izzy, not the ladder. I mean, yes the ladder, but . . . my arm," Zack winced.

Izzy knelt down next to her brother and put a hand on his shoulder. "Don't move, Zack," she said, her voice shaking. "I'm going to get Mom."

"Wait, don't leave me," Zack cried, but Izzy was already running to the house.

Izzy opened the back door to yell into the house, "Mom! Hurry!" she yelled. "Zack fell out of the old willow tree and broke his arm!"

In moments, Izzy's mom, Scarlet Philips, burst out of the house and raced past her. Cody, Mrs. Philips's friend-who-was-quickly-becoming-a-boyfriend, followed closely behind. Together, they found Zack lying under the tree and moaning softly.

Mrs. Philips took one look at Zack and gasped. She kneeled at his side and yelled, "Izzy, call Mrs. Clark and ask her to come right away!" Mrs. Clark lived right down the street and worked as an emergency room nurse.

Mrs. Clark arrived within minutes and went straight to Zack. Brooke, Mrs. Clark's daughter, had tagged along and stood by Izzy to watch. The two girls differed both in personality and in style—Izzy was quieter, wore plain outfits, and tied her long, straight, brown hair back in a ponytail while Brooke had wild, curly hair and loved to dress in bold, brightly colored outfits— but they were best friends. They spent so much time with each other that Zack was like a brother to Brooke, and she wanted to make sure he was okay, too.

"Can you describe what happened and tell me what hurts?" Mrs. Clark asked Zack while looking into his eyes and then checking his pulse and breathing.

4

"I was climbing the ladder, trying to see into the woodpecker hole. I was being careful, but . . . then the ladder broke," Zack described slowly.

"Did you get a look at her nestlings?" Cody, who had taught Zack much of what he knew about birds, asked.

Mrs. Philips frowned at Cody and said, "How can you worry about seeing baby birds when his arm looks broken and he could have a concussion—or worse?"

Cody looked at Zack and realized he was pale and shaking. Cody kneeled down to put a hand on his shoulder. "You're right, I guess I am a little overly bird-centric," Cody said. He then looked at Mrs. Clark and asked, "How is he?"

Mrs. Clark looked up from assessing Zack's injuries and smiled reassuringly at Scarlet and Cody. "The good news is, I don't believe he injured his head or back, but he certainly does have a broken arm."

Mrs. Philips let out a deep breath. "Thank you so much, Nicole."

"Of course! He doesn't need an ambulance. As soon as I'm done stabilizing his arm, you can drive him to the hospital. If you want, I can drive with you or watch Carson."

Izzy and Zack's little brother Carson was still a toddler and was napping inside, oblivious to all the commotion.

"Actually, if you could take both Carson *and* Izzy to your house, I'd really appreciate it."

"But Mom," Izzy said, "I want to go to the hospital with you!"

"Oh honey," Mrs. Philips said, "you'd have so much more fun at Brooke's house."

"What if Zack needs me?"

"Come on, Izzy," Brooke urged, pulling on Izzy's arm. "We can make popcorn and watch movies and you can sleep over!"

"Wait," Zack said, suddenly perking up from his daze. "You're going to watch movies and eat popcorn while I go to the hospital? That's not fair. I want to watch movies, too!"

"Hmm. He seems to be doing better already,"

Izzy noted with a laugh. "And watching movies does sound pretty good. But Mom, will you call me every fifteen minutes with an update?"

"I'll keep you updated every few hours," Mrs. Philips promised. "Unfortunately, hospital visits tend to be very slow. We might be there all night waiting for Zack to get his arm set in a cast."

"A cast? I can't have a cast! I need my arm for the Green County swim-a-thon next week! The Nature Club needs me!" Zack cried.

Mrs. Philips knew how much Zack loved being part of the Nature Club. Izzy, Zack, Brooke, and their friend Tai had formed the club earlier that summer. The goals of the club were to learn about nature and to take action to protect it. Izzy's pen pal in Nicaragua, Miguel, was even a member from afar.

Mrs. Philips also knew how excited Zack was about the swim-a-thon. Izzy, Zack, Brooke, and Tai had entered the Nature Club as one of the five, four-person teams participating to raise money for their favorite cause: Green County Park.

"Zack, I'm so sorry. Maybe Izzy could take over your pledges and apply them to her laps."

"But Mom, it's a team event. Each pledge already applies to everyone on the team's laps added together—not just to the laps of the person who collected that pledge. They need my laps. I'm going to let everyone down!"

Zack, who hadn't cried throughout the whole ordeal of breaking his arm, now broke down sobbing. Izzy brought Zack his favorite stuffed penguin to try and cheer him up while Mrs. Clark stabilized his arm and his mother went inside to prepare an overnight bag. When she returned, Cody carried Zack to the car, and they set off to the hospital.

2

At the hospital, Mrs. Philips and Cody brought Zack into a special waiting room just for kids. It was bright and cheery and stocked with books, games, and puzzles. A woman stood quietly in the corner rocking her sleeping baby, but then a nurse called her in, so they had the place to themselves.

Zack loved puzzles but was in no shape to do one, so Cody entertained him with magic tricks. When a nurse finally came for Zack, he had forgotten about the swim-a-thon and was no longer feeling pain.

Zack stayed upbeat throughout the nurse's exam and x-rays, entertained by the beeping monitors, flashing lights, and general hectic energy of the hospital but he tensed back up when the doctor arrived. The doctor, a woman with long blond hair tied back in a low ponytail, was all business. Looking and speaking directly to Zack, she said, "I'm Dr. Carter. Please tell me what happened."

Zack stared at her wide-eyed without saying a word. Normally quiet, he talked even less around unfamiliar adults.

"Honey, you need to tell the doctor what happened," his mother said gently.

"I wanted to see the birds," Zack said quietly. "But I couldn't see them."

Dr. Carter looked at Mrs. Philips and Cody. "What's he talking about?" she asked.

Since Cody was the less anxious of the two, he jumped in. "This little nature kid wanted to look into a woodpecker's nest high up on the trunk of an old willow tree. He climbed up a rickety old ladder to get a good look when a cracked rung on the ladder broke and down he went. He had some bad luck, but also some good luck, since he didn't hurt his back or head—just his arm," Cody concluded, smiling at Zack.

"He was very lucky." Dr. Carter paused and looked directly at Zack. "He could have been hurt much worse and there is an important lesson to be learned. That is, his accident could easily have been prevented."

Zack's mouth dropped open and he looked to his mom for help.

"It was my fault," Mrs. Philips said to Dr. Carter. "I've been meaning to get that ladder fixed since we moved in last month. You see, we are just renting the place, so it wasn't a huge priority and well, I just haven't had time . . . ." She paused and looked at Zack. "I'm so sorry, honey."

"No, Mom," Zack jumped in, suddenly willing to speak to defend his mother. "You're a great mom. You said not to use the ladder. But I . . . ," Zack looked down. "I used it anyway." Zack's eyes filled with tears.

"Listen, at this point, there's no use looking for blame," Dr. Carter said. "But there's a lot of use thinking about how to prevent another accident."

"We will do that," Mrs. Philips promised, but

Dr. Carter wasn't done with her lecture.

"Mrs. Philips, it's worth taking the time to clean up other potential hazards around your house. For your kids' safety—and your own—you simply have to take care of your environment. And Zack, please take what your mother says more seriously in the future."

Zack gulped and sat quietly while his mother, turning slightly red, said, "We absolutely will."

"Good," said Dr. Carter. "Now, Zack, I can tell from your x-rays you don't need surgery, but I do have to reset your arm."

It wasn't until the doctor said "reset" that Zack even considered that more pain was coming.

"Reset?" he asked hesitantly.

"Yes. I need to make sure the bones are in their correct places so they grow back together properly. You don't want a crooked arm, do you?" Dr. Carter bluntly asked.

Before Zack could answer, Dr. Carter took a firm hold of his arm and set the bones back into their correct places.

Zack screamed out from the sudden pain, but almost immediately stopped after realizing the pain had already come and gone. He looked up and saw Dr. Carter smiling at him.

"Well done, off you go," Dr. Carter said. She turned and quickly disappeared down the hall.

Then a cheerful nurse pushed Zack down the hall in a wheelchair to the casting room where she introduced him to a short, stout man with a Yankees cap and wire-rimmed glasses. "This is Max. He will wrap your arm and give you instructions for its care," she said before leaving.

"Welcome to Max's casting! You must be Zack," Max said enthusiastically. "Since you can't grow a new arm, I'm going to wrap your broken one in a splint so it can heal."

"Did you hear that, Mom? I don't need a cast," Zack said with a smile.

"Hold on there, partner. You will only have the splint for about five days to let the swelling go down. Then you need to come back for a cast."

"I do need a cast?" Zack asked, his eyes filling

13

with tears again.

"Oh yes. In fact, you'll be wearing that cast for the next six weeks," Max explained.

"Six weeks?" Zack repeated.

"That sounds like forever, doesn't it? Now tell me what you're going to miss while you're wearing a fantastic new cast."

"I'll miss the swim-a-thon," Zack said. "I can't miss the swim-a-thon."

Max listened carefully as Zack told him about the Nature Club and how they had organized the event. He explained how they planned to raise money so the park could fix the wooden, split-rail fence that protects its most fragile meadow.

"It sure does sound like they need you," Max said. "Perhaps your penguin can swim for you."

Zack clutched his penguin tighter as he explained, "Otto can't swim. He isn't real."

"Ah, I didn't know," Max teased. "But I can tell you're a clever kid. I bet you'll come up with a way to still be part of the swim-a-thon. Penguin or no penguin.

"Now," Max continued, changing the subject. "How about if you pick a good color for your cast now, and I'll save it for you for when you come back. How about blue? Or purple? Or camouflage?" Max showed Zack samples of each color of casting plaster. "What color will make you happy?"

Zack knew exactly what color he wanted, "Can I have orange?" he asked with a hint of a smile.

"Excellent choice!" Max said. "Are you an Orioles fan? Bengals?" Zack just smiled.

"Hmmm. It must be a college team. Is it Syracuse?" Zack continued to smile.

"Okay. I give up. Why the orange?"

"Orange is a happy color," Zack answered, now smiling fully.

"You know what?" Max said. "You're right. Orange is, indeed, a happy color." Max set the orange aside, wrapped Zack's arm in a splint, and then gave him explicit instructions for its care, the most important one being: "*Don't get it wet.*"

It was so late when they got back that when

Mrs. Philips stopped by the Clarks' house to pick up Izzy and Carson, they were already sound asleep, so she left them to finish the night there.

At home, the kitchen was a mess—there were unwashed dishes and unfinished art projects covering everything. Too tired to pick up, Mrs. Philips microwaved frozen burritos and they ate them in the living room.

As they ate, Cody said, "As soon as I get time, I'll fix that ladder."

"That sounds great," Mrs. Philips said.

"I want to help, too," Zack said, yawning.

Cody looked at Zack's broken arm and raising one eyebrow, said, "Right."

"I'd better put our little champ here to bed," Mrs. Philips said to Cody. "Thanks for your help."

"Anytime."

Cody let himself out as Mrs. Philips scooped Zack up, carried him upstairs, and got him ready for bed. She then picked out a book to read to him, but before she even started reading, he was sound asleep.

3

The next morning, Mrs. Philips looked around her messy kitchen for sugar to put in her coffee when Mrs. Clark called. "Hi Nicole," Mrs. Philips greeted her groggily.

"Hi Scarlet. How's Zack?"

"Well, you were right," Mrs. Philips yawned. "He broke his arm, but he's otherwise fine."

"How's he taking it?" Mrs. Clark asked.

"The pain doesn't seem to be bothering him at all. I think his biggest disappointment is missing the swim-a-thon. He's been so excited about it."

"Poor kid," Mrs. Clark said. "But don't worry. He's adaptable."

"You're right. And thanks for checking in."

"Of course. And hey, the girls are about to head over with Carson."

"Sounds good. Can you please send some sugar

with them? I can't find ours," Mrs. Philips asked.

"Absolutely," Mrs. Clark answered. "How's your rental house working out?"

"I feel lucky we found it, but I've been so busy that I never took the time to unpack. It's also hard to get motivated to fully unpack since I'll just have to pack it all back up at the end of the summer. The problem is, I now have a mess." The Philipses had moved from Green County to Southern California last fall but came back to Green County for the summer to be closer to Mrs. Philips' mother, Izzy and Zack's Grandma Pearl.

"I can imagine," Mrs. Clark said. "Working and taking care of three kids by yourself must be exhausting. I'll come and help you get organized."

"Excellent! I'll make you dinner in return."

"It's a deal. Talk to you later."

"Bye."

A few minutes after they hung up, Izzy and Brooke burst in the front door with Carson and a container of sugar.

"How's Zack?" Brooke and Izzy asked at the

same time.

Before Mrs. Philips could answer, Zack yelled, "I got a splint and in five days—actually now just four—I'll get an orange cast," while running down the stairs in his pajamas.

"Orange? Fantastic!" Brooke exclaimed. "Can we sign it when you get it?"

"Are you okay? Did it hurt?" Izzy added.

"Yes, you can sign it and yes, it hurt," Zack said, beaming.

"The only thing is, now I can't do the swim-a-thon," Zack said, no longer smiling.

"I'm afraid it'll be six weeks before he can get back in the water," his mom added.

Izzy's mouth dropped open and Brooke asked, "Can't he just wrap his arm in a plastic bag?"

"Can I?" asked Zack, his eyes lighting up.

"I'm sorry Zack," Mrs. Philips answered, "but when the man gave you the splint—"

"Max," Zack interrupted.

"Right," his mother continued. "When Max gave you the splint, he was clear that the splint—

and the cast that follows—have got to stay completely dry."

"Sorry, Zack," Izzy muttered.

"Yeah, that really stinks," Brooke added.

"What are you kids going to do today?" Mrs. Philips asked, changing the subject.

"We're, uh . . . we're about to head over to meet Tai at the park and, uh . . . and swim in the creek," Izzy answered awkwardly. Can Zack still come but just put his feet in?"

"Can I, Mom?" he asked.

"Yes. But please, be careful."

Zack ran upstairs to get dressed while Izzy and her mom prepared a big red beach bag with towels, sunscreen, water, the kids' nature journals, and snacks.

"Izzy, I think everything you need is in here— except your goggles. Where are they?" Mrs. Philips asked.

"I have no idea. I can't find them anywhere," Izzy replied.

"If only there was enough time in the day to

get all this organized," Mrs. Philips sighed. "Don't worry. I'm sure we'll find your goggles before the swim-a-thon."

A few minutes later, Zack reappeared in the kitchen wearing flip-flops, shorts, and his favorite orange T-shirt wrapped around his neck. "I guess I need some help," he said.

Mrs. Philips laughed and fixed his shirt. "Okay, he's ready. Have fun at the park and yell if you need anything," she told them. I'll have the window open so I can listen for you."

Mrs. Philips sat down to finally enjoy her coffee as the three kids ran down the street to the park. Green County Park was their favorite place. Izzy and Zack's old house—the one they had lived in before moving to Southern California—was right next to the park, but they were pretty happy to be able to rent one for the summer that was just down the street.

Tai, who lived a bit farther away and usually biked over, was already there. As the others approached, he tipped back his cowboy hat and grinned at Zack. "Well, I'll be darned. You really did go and break your arm. How'd you fall out of that tree, anyhow?"

Zack, who usually just followed along and hardly ever spoke, was now enjoying all the attention from the older kids. He told Tai about the fall, his hospital visit, and picking out orange for his cast.

"Wow. That was a big adventure," Tai said when Zack finished. "You're one brave kid."

Zack beamed at the compliment. Then Tai added, "It's too bad you can't do the swim-a-thon. I bet you would've done a hundred laps."

"I can't do one hundred, but I could've done at least thirty," Zack said, his smile quickly fading.

Izzy put her arm around her little brother and said, "There will be other swim-a-thons. The main thing is that you'll be okay."

***

While the older kids went for a swim in the creek, Zack grabbed his journal from the bag and found a shady spot to sit on a rock and sketch. For a six-year-old, he was pretty good at sitting still— as long as he was outside.

As the others laughed and splashed around, Zack peered into the water where a pond had formed beside the creek. Right away, he spotted his favorite insects—water striders. Zack envied their ability to walk across the top of the water.

When he squatted to get a closer look, he noticed a cluster of about eighty clear eggs with large dark centers. They were attached to some grass at the edge of the pond with a clear, jelly-like substance. Examining them closely, he saw dark forms within them wiggling. *Tadpoles?* he wondered. On further inspection, he found they were indeed tiny tadpoles, as some had hatched out of their eggs and were swimming about.

Beyond the tiny tadpoles, he then found even bigger tadpoles that must have hatched several days earlier. They were brown on top and lighter on the bottom, had wide upper bodies and skinny tails, and had big googly eyes. Even more amazing, some of them had back legs!

23

When he leaned in to look more closely, he realized one of the tadpoles had a piece of nylon fishing line wrapped around its back left leg.

"Oh no!" he said out loud and then thought, *I can help it*. Zack sat perfectly still while moving his right hand closer and closer to the tadpole until suddenly, *splash!* He caught it.

It felt wet and cold as it flopped about in his hand. Zack examined it and saw the fishing line caused its leg to bend oddly. He then transferred the tadpole to his left hand—at least the part of his hand that was sticking out of the splint—so he could use his right one to remove the fishing line. "One, two, three" he counted and quickly pulled it off.

He knew the tadpole needed to return to the water to breathe, but he wasn't quite done inspecting it, so he held onto it and just dipped it into the water. *Splash!* "Oh no!" Zack cried, realizing in that moment that he'd done it with his *left* arm—the one in the splint.

Looking at the tadpole, he said to it, "You're

lucky you don't have to stay dry. My mom's going to kill me."

Sighing, Zack turned back to inspecting the tadpole. He loved the whole idea of metamorphosis—an animal changing from one form into another—and was excited to see one actually in the process of it. It frustrated Zack when animals changed in secret, like when caterpillars pupated into butterflies hidden within a chrysalis.

It was then that Zack noticed something he hadn't seen earlier since he'd been so focused on the fishing line. "Hey, Izzy! Brooke! Tai!" Zack suddenly yelled. "You've got to see this!"

4

The injured tadpole flopped about in Zack's hand. The tadpole's quick dip back into the creek had given him a chance to fill up on oxygen—tadpoles use gills to pull oxygen right out of the water rather than lungs to breathe oxygen from the air like adult frogs—but now he needed more and struggled frantically to get back into the water.

This was just another bump in an already turbulent day. It didn't start off that way. He'd had a relatively quiet morning hidden in the plants at the bottom of the creek. There, he was safe from the hungry jaws of predators, which included everything from snakes to herons and even to adult frogs of his own species.

He had spent several hours hidden away until—like the predators stalking him—he, too, needed something to eat. Back before he'd started growing legs and arms—or changing into a frog at all—he'd had rows of tiny teeth he would use to feed on algae attached to the rocks at the bottom of the creek.

Now that he was transforming, he no longer had those teeth. In fact, along with the rest of his body, his entire mouth was rearranging, so there was little he could actually eat. One exception was pollen, since he could just swallow it, but it was all floating at the top of the water.

To get it, he would have to leave his safe hiding spot. After a few hours of hiding, he got hungry enough to swim to the surface to nibble on the floating pollen.

It was then and there that his day changed for the worse. But it wasn't a predator that got him; rather, it was a piece of nylon fishing line that somehow became wrapped around his back left leg. And there it stayed until a large creature reached into the water and grabbed him.

While that very large creature's grabbing him led to his being freed from the fishing line, it was now keeping him from the water where he needed to be to breathe. Fearful he would suffocate, he flopped about, trying to get back into the water. It was right then that the very large creature let out a very loud yell.

5

Izzy, Brooke, and Tai rushed over to Zack.

"Are you okay?" Izzy asked breathlessly as she splashed out of the water toward him, with Brooke and Tai right behind her.

"This. Is. Amazing," Zack said slowly, without even looking up at them. "Not only does this thing have a tail and back legs growing in, but it even has the start of front legs!"

"Whoa, that *is* amazing," Tai said, dripping all over Zack as he looked at the tadpole flopping about in Zack's hand.

"Seriously!" added Brooke.

Izzy, however, wasn't looking at the tadpole and wasn't smiling. She was staring at Zack's wet splint. "Your arm!" Izzy cried. "You splint is going to be ruined."

"Izzy," Tai interrupted, "his splint isn't ruined.

It's just a little wet."

"A little wet?" Izzy asked. "Mom's going to kill him. And me."

"You're exaggerating, Izzy," Brooke said. "She might be mad, but she won't be that mad. And seriously, this tadpole is crazy looking. You have to see it. This little guy is actually growing new arms! Imagine if Zack could just grow a new arm."

"This tadpole isn't growing new arms. It's growing its first set of arms," Izzy corrected her while finally joining the others to take a look.

"This crazy-looking thing is a tadpole going through metamorphosis?" Brooke asked.

"Yup," Zack answered.

"What kind of salamander is it going to become?" Tai asked.

"Actually, it will become a frog," Zack said.

"Whoa. How'd you know that?" Tai asked.

"We watched tadpoles like this turn into frogs in a fish tank at school," Zack said without looking up from the creek.

"Frogs are so much cuter than tadpoles,"

Brooke observed. "That thing is kind of gross."

"It is," Izzy agreed. "But it's also kind of awesome. I wish Miguel could see it. He writes about frogs almost as much as he writes about birds and soccer. He calls them *ranas*. He says that *rana* is Spanish for frog."

"Then I'm going to name this one Rana," Zack said with a smile.

"Cool name," Brooke commented.

"I think Rana wants to get back in that water to breathe," Tai said.

"You're right," Zack said, looking down at it. Then he whispered, "Good luck," and released the tadpole back into the water. The tadpole wiggled at first and then dove under some vegetation.

"It looks like one of its legs is crooked or something," Brooke said.

"There was fishing line wrapped around its leg. I took it off," Zack explained.

"Good job, Zack. That's so sad. I hope it can still become a healthy frog," Izzy worried aloud.

"Me too. I wonder what kind of frog it's

becoming," Brooke said.

"I've got a book about reptiles and amphibians in my room," Zack said to Izzy.

"Then let's go to our house and look it up," Izzy said to the group.

"Great. Are there good snacks at your house?" Tai asked.

"Seriously!" Brooke added. "I'm starving."

"Yes. But before we go, we should write down everything we can about these tadpoles in our journals so we can look it up in Zack's book," Izzy suggested.

"I'm too hungry to write," Zack said.

"Then we will have to memorize the traits," Izzy said.

They discussed all the tadpoles' defining traits and then Izzy said, "Okay, Zack, why don't you review the list of what we found and then we can head home."

"They are totally awesome," Zack started.

"Yes, they are," Izzy agreed. "What else?"

"They are kind of brownish, their tails are kind

of clear, and they have an awesome stripe that goes across their faces—even right through their eyes. And . . . ," Zack paused to examine them again, "their legs and arms are starting to grow!"

"I've got the brownish color," Tai offered.

"I'll remember about the stripe," Brooke said. "That is totally cool. Someone else can deal with the new legs and arms."

"Why?" Tai asked. "Don't you want to dream about being half-tadpole and half-person?" he said while making a crazy face and waving his arms around.

"That is so creepy!" Brooke yelled, running away from him.

They used that momentum to get moving and run to Izzy and Zack's house.

When they walked in the door, Mrs. Philips greeted them with a plate of apple slices dipped in honey.

Zack, who had carefully hidden his wet splint from his mother as he walked into the house, completely forgot about it as he ran up to grab a slice of apple. "Um, Zack," said Mrs. Philips, looking at him crossly. "Is there something you want to tell me?"

"It wasn't my fault," he started. "I had to keep the tadpole alive."

Mrs. Philips didn't even ask about what he was saying. She was used to Zack and Izzy's adventures at Green County Park and just rolled her eyes. "Just don't complain to me when it starts to itch."

"Itch?" asked Zack.

"And stink," added Mrs. Philips.

"Itch and stink?" Zack asked.

Giggling at the look of horror on Zack's face, Brooke said, "Let's go look at Zack's book."

Mrs. Philips smiled knowingly, shaking her head. She then added, "You kids have fun. Just remember Carson is taking a nap in his room," and went back to reading. Carson was only three and still took afternoon naps—luckily, he could sleep through a lot of noise and commotion.

As the kids headed off, Izzy whispered, "Sorry

Mom," to Mrs. Philips.

Once they were inside with the door closed, they started laughing again while Zack looked around his room for the field guide. Although he had a bookshelf, not many books were on it—instead, they were spread around his room and mixed into piles of games, stuffed animals, and dirty clothes. Zack remembered looking through the book the week before while lying on his bed, but he just couldn't find it.

"Zack, this is disgusting. How can you live like this?" Izzy asked with her hands on her hips.

"Sorry," Zack told the others, "I can't find it. Maybe when I clean my room, I'll find it. If not, I'm going to the library tomorrow. I'll check another one out and then we can look it up."

"Sounds good to me. I already forgot what I was supposed to remember anyway," Tai said.

"Not me," Brooke said. "That tadpole had the coolest stripe ever."

"Actually, not me either," Zack said. "Rana was awesome!"

6

The next day, the group returned to the creek after Zack checked out the book from the library.

"Here they are!" Zack yelled after spotting them. "Their front arms are bigger and their tails are smaller than even yesterday. They're so close to becoming frogs!"

"I'll be darned," Tai said.

Izzy flipped through Zack's book until finally saying, "Aha!"

"What are they becoming?" Brooke asked impatiently.

"Pacific chorus frogs," Izzy said. "It says they used to be called Pacific tree frogs, even though they don't really climb trees, and that they are sometimes called striped chorus frogs because they have a dark stripe from the tip of their nose toward their shoulder."

"That stripe is just so stylish," Brooke said.

Izzy laughed. "They do still seem to have a sense of style. The book says they come in a range of colors and can even change colors to blend into the background."

"Oh right, I was supposed to remember his color, but as it turns out, it didn't even matter since they can change color," Tai said.

Leaning over Izzy to look at the book, Brooke said, "It also says they have big, cool-looking toepads for climbing,"

"You've got to be kidding that the book says, 'cool-looking'?" Tai said.

"Well, no. I added that part because they are cool looking, right?" Brooke asked.

"Way cool!" Zack agreed.

"It also says that once a tadpole has back legs, it's called a 'metamorph,' and then once it has front legs, it's called a 'froglet.'" Izzy read.

"Oh, come on," Brooke said. "That's so cute. Zack, we need to call your little friend a froglet, not a tadpole."

"Or we could call him *Pseudacris regilla* because it says here that's his Latin name," Izzy suggested.

"Um. No way," Brooke said.

"Actually, we need to call him Rana, because that's his name," Zack said, looking downcast. "I feel so bad for Rana. He can't get a cast like I did. How can we make sure no other froglets, frogs, metamorphs, *or* tadpoles get hurt like Rana did?"

"How about if we, the Nature Club, spend some time looking for fish hooks and fishing line and get rid of them?" Izzy suggested. "We normally spend time picking up trash anyway, so why not?"

"Good idea, but I've hardly ever even seen fishing line or hooks in Green Creek," Tai said.

"I think we just need to train our eyes to them," Brooke suggested. "My mom says I can find purple and sparkles like no one else because I zero in on them."

Izzy, Tai, and Zack all looked over at Brooke and laughed. She was wearing a purple tank top with red leggings topped off with a silver belt and purple sparkly glasses. "You do have a point," Tai commented. "Let's try for half an hour."

When everyone agreed, Tai set his watch alarm and they got started. Almost immediately, Tai found fishing line tangled in a tree, and Izzy pulled some line with a hook at the end from the creek. Brooke picked up three broken rubber lures she found in the mud. After that, it was slower going, but they did pick up trash and three more tangled masses of fishing line.

Zack, who hadn't yet found anything, decided to scan all the tadpoles, metamorphs, and froglets to see if any of the others had fishing line wrapped around their legs. That was when he noticed the water along the edges of the creek had a shiny, rainbow-colored reflection from the sun. Mesmerized, he again yelled to the others.

"Slow down, partner. We still have seven minutes," Tai yelled back.

"But you've got to see this," Zack said.

Again, Tai and Brooke gathered around Zack

to see what he'd found. At first, they didn't see anything, but then Brooke said, "Why is the water so colorful here?"

"Yeah, why?" Zack added.

"What are you guys looking at?" Izzy asked, joining them.

"What we're looking at is an oil spill," Tai answered.

"Oil?" Brooke asked.

"He's right," Izzy confirmed. "I've seen it when my mom changes out the oil in our car."

"But why would there be oil in the creek?" Brooke asked.

"I don't know, but we'd better find out. Those poor tadpoles—I mean froglets—could get sick and die. If there is oil in the water, they won't be able to breathe," Izzy answered.

"Oh no!" cried Zack. "I better take Rana home with me."

"I don't know, Zack," said Izzy. "I think Rana is one of the few that might be able to get out. It's the tadpoles and metamorphs that are stuck in the creek."

"Then I'll take all of them home," he said.

"You're going to need one huge tank for them to live in," said Brooke. "Or a lot of buckets."

"We have buckets in our garage!" Zack remembered.

"I don't know," said Izzy, biting her bottom lip. "Mom might not like it."

"But we can't let them die!" Zack cried.

Izzy looked at her brother's anguished face and said, "Okay, let's go home and get some buckets. I'm pretty sure there's at least three in the garage."

"I think we have some nets in my basement," Brooke said. "How about if we all get what we need and meet back here in fifteen minutes?"

"Izzy and Brooke, what if you two round up the buckets and nets while I sit here with Zack to keep an eye on the spill?" Tai suggested.

"And on Rana," Zack added.

"Great," Brooke answered while Izzy nodded in agreement. The girls ran off, leaving Tai and

Zack at the creek.

"I'll start catching them," said Zack. "Then we can put them in the buckets when Izzy and Brooke get back."

"Hold on there," Tai urged. "There's no sense in that. They could dry out and suffocate. How 'bout we sit and track them until the others get back? Then we'll use the nets to catch them and put them in the buckets."

"Right. Good point," agreed Zack.

Zack and Tai set up an observation area, and Zack quickly got comfortable. Or so he thought. As soon as he was sitting still, he felt an itch from deep within his splint.

7

The oil in the creek continued to spread. At first, Rana took no notice of it. He was sitting at the bottom of the creek next to a large rock. He wasn't hiding under the leaf litter this time, but he was still well hidden because as a froglet, he could easily camouflage with his background.

Eventually though, Rana swam up to the surface to feed on more pollen. When he did, he came into contact with the oil. The oil felt different from the water both in temperature and texture, and he climbed up onto a rock near the edge of the creek to get away from it. Sitting on the rock, he quickly gulped air into his newly formed lungs.

There he sat in the silence, warming his body in the sun and gulping in more air. He moved around a bit, but was somewhat unsteady, as his left leg bent at an unusual angle. He put most of his weight on his right leg and tried using his left for stability.

Suddenly, he was startled by the sound of people laughing and walking toward him. He quickly splashed back into the creek where he could hide and wait for the danger to pass.

8

Zack was trying to shove a stick into his splint to scratch his itch when he heard the girls returning. "Finally," he muttered.

"We were really fast, weren't we?" Brooke called out.

"Like a herd of turtles," Tai teased.

"Actually, it's a bale of turtles," Zack corrected him.

"Turtles? You mean a bale of frogs," Brooke teased back.

"That would be an *army* of frogs," Zack said.

"How's Rana?" Izzy asked, changing the topic.

"Zack's little buddy crawled up on that rock for a bit," Tai said. "Then he plopped back into the water and is now tucked under those leaves. He's kind of off to the left of the edge of the spill."

Zack pointed to the spot, and the others got

down on their hands and knees to try and see him. They became so focused on looking that they jumped when they heard, "Izzy, Tai, Brooke, Zack! How are you kids?"

When they looked up, they saw Victoria Perez walking toward them. She was wearing her standard brown county parks uniform and as always, had her thick black hair in a long braid down her back.

"Hi, Victoria!" the group said in unison.

Victoria was the biologist who had taught them to keep human food and trash away from wildlife after a bear had gotten into the trash at Brooke's house. But that time, she had been with two other biologists named Logan and Cameron. Today, she had someone else with her: a tall man with curly brown hair and black glasses. Instead of wearing a uniform, he was wearing a T-shirt that said, "Frogs make me hoppy."

"Kids, I want you to meet Daniel. He's an aquatic ecologist. He studies the interaction of life within the aquatic world. Daniel, these are the kids I told you about with the Nature Club."

"Hi," the kids said at the same time.

"What are you doing?" Brooke asked.

"I'm doing a survey for aquatic insects," Daniel said. "My favorites are the stoneflies. They indicate good water quality because they only live in clean, cool streams."

"If only it was a clean stream," Izzy said.

"What do you mean?" Daniel asked. "And what are you doing with all those buckets?"

"Oh my gosh, it's crazy," Brooke said. "There's an oil spill, and it's going to make all the tadpoles and froglets suffocate, so we're catching them to take them to Izzy and Zack's house where they'll be safe."

"Except Rana. We think he can get away," Zack added. "And we didn't know about the stoneflies before. Now we have to worry about them, too."

Noticing Daniel's surprised expression, Brooke jumped in and explained how Zack had found a froglet with fishing line wrapped around its leg, and how he'd named it Rana. She explained that

Zack had removed the fishing line, but Rana's leg was still bent, and he may have to grow a new one. "Then we searched the creek for fishing line and hooks to save Rana's friends from the same fate," Brooke explained.

"Only now, they might die in the oil," Zack added from afar. He was pacing back and forth in the meadow beside the creek, trying to distract himself from the itchiness inside his splint.

"It's fantastic that you saved Rana and the others from getting tangled, but . . . ," Daniel paused dramatically until he got Zack's attention. "You don't want to harm him now by trampling his habitat. This is the area the Nature Club is trying to protect." When Zack didn't react, Daniel added, "You know, trying to protect by raising money to repair the fence . . . the fence that is meant to keep people from trampling the meadow."

Blushing, Zack quickly hopped out of the meadow. "Ooops."

"I never made the connection about why the

meadow needed the fence until this very moment!" Brooke said.

"That's okay, most people don't. That's why we use an actual fence and not just signs in our most fragile areas," Daniel said.

"Can't people just climb over it?" Tai asked.

"They can. Or they can go under it. And that's okay. We purposely picked a split-rail style of fence over a wire or chain-link fence so we don't keep animals from being able to get past it. Some people will get past it, but we are at least giving the message to most people that this is a protected area we don't want humans to trample," Daniel explained. "I also want to talk for a second about something else you said—about Rana growing a new leg. Like us, Rana only gets one set of legs."

"You sure?" Tai asked.

"I am," Daniel answered. "There's only one amphibian that can lose an arm or leg and then regrow it—and it's not a frog, it's a rare salamander called an axolotl. It can even regrow parts of its brain."

"But all salamanders can regrow their tails, right?" Brooke asked.

"You're thinking about lizards. If a predator grabs a lizard's tail, the tail can break off so the lizard can escape. It can then grow a new one."

"Wait a minute. I'm getting confused. What's the difference between a salamander and a lizard?" Brooke asked.

"Salamanders are amphibians and lizards are reptiles," Izzy said. "I read about it."

"Then what's the difference between an amphibian and a reptile?" Brooke asked.

"How about if I start by telling you what they have in common?" Daniel asked. The kids nodded. "They're all vertebrates, meaning they have backbones. And they're all cold-blooded, meaning their body temperature isn't regulated internally, like ours."

"Okay, now what's different?" Brooke asked.

"Amphibians start as tadpoles and breathe through gills like fish. Then they metamorphose into adult frogs, toads, newts, or salamanders with moist, smooth skin. As adults, they have lungs, so they live on land, but they still go to water to lay their eggs. Your frog, Rana, is an amphibian."

"Got it," Tai said. "Now, what about the reptiles?"

"Reptiles all have scales—or scutes, in the case of turtles—and as they age, they don't change form, they just get bigger," Daniel said. "Reptiles include lizards, turtles, alligators, crocodiles, and snakes. When they are adults, they have dry, scaly skin, and they lay their eggs on land."

"Okay. Got it," Tai said.

"Me too," Brooke added.

"I already knew that," Zack said to Izzy.

"Now, to the problem at hand—the oil," Daniel continued. "You say you want to save the tadpoles and metamorphs by catching them, but where do you plan to put them after you catch them?" Daniel asked.

"In our garage," Zack said.

"And then what?" Daniel asked.

"And then . . . take care of them," Zack said.

"Hmmm. Did you brainstorm any other ideas?" Daniel asked.

"Nope," Tai said. "The garage was all we came up with."

"Why? What should we do?" Izzy asked.

"I suggest you don't move them. Unless there is a really good reason—animals should always be left alone."

"It seems like the oil is a really good reason. Isn't it?" Brooke asked.

"The oil is a problem, but it's a little spill, and we have people in the county trained to divert it and clean it up."

"I'll call right now to get them mobilized," Victoria said, pulling out her phone and stepping away from the group.

"But what will happen to Rana's friends? Are you *sure* we shouldn't catch and move them?" Zack asked.

"I am sure. Taking animals into captivity

should always be your last option. Imagine if we had to leave our amazing Earth and instead go and live on Mars. It just doesn't make sense. We are always better off taking care of our environment than trying to find a new one. If this was a bigger oil spill, we would have to move them, but since it is a little one, and we can get most of it cleaned up, they should be okay."

"Okay team, a crew is coming," Victoria said as she returned to the group.

"How do they know how to clean it up?" Brooke asked.

"Unfortunately, they get a lot of practice. These little spills happen a lot," Victoria said, shaking her head.

"Where is it coming from and why does it keep happening?" Izzy asked.

"It's coming from drains throughout the watershed."

"What's a watershed?" Zack whispered to Izzy.

"A watershed is an area of land within which all the creeks and streams drain into the same body of water. In this case, Green Creek," Daniel, who overheard, explained.

"Since the watershed contains our whole town, it's coming from storm drains throughout our town," Victoria added.

"What are storm drains?" Zack asked, directly to Daniel this time.

"They are the drains on the sides of the roads. They allow storm water to get to the creek. You know, they look like grates on the sides of the road. The problem is that it isn't just water that goes into the drains. Oil, chemicals, and anything else that spills onto the streets also make their way into the drains and therefore the creek, and even worse, careless people dump all kinds of things into the drains."

"Those drain into the creek? How would anyone know that?" Brooke asked.

"Doesn't everyone know that?" Victoria asked.

"I didn't," Zack said. "Did you know, Tai?"

"Nope. But I never really thought about it before," Tai said.

"Interesting," Victoria observed. "Maybe the people who are dumping oil aren't being negligent. Maybe they're making an honest mistake."

"Maybe we can stop people from doing it by teaching them that the drains lead to Green Creek," Izzy said.

"Right," Tai agreed. "If people knew, they wouldn't dump oil in there."

"I really do hope you're right. It's hard to believe anyone would intentionally pollute the creek," Victoria said.

"What if we put up a sign near each drain?" Zack said.

"Great idea. We could paint information right on the curbs next to each drain," Izzy said.

"We could use purple paint with glitter!" Brooke added.

"Zack, that is a very good idea," Daniel said. "Many towns paint messages near the drains— something like, 'drains to creek' with a picture of a fish. And, as Brooke suggested, purple would be fine—just maybe not the glitter."

"Don't you like glitter?" Brooke asked.

"Oh, I love how glitter livens things up," Daniel answered. "Unfortunately, most types of glitter are made from tiny pieces of plastic that can get into the water and harm the fish."

"Ohhhh nooooo," Brooke said slowly. "I can't imagine life without glitter."

"So, can we do it—but without the glitter?" Zack asked.

"Yes," Victoria answered. "Your contact will be Janet Helling at the Green County office. I believe she was the one who helped you protect milkweeds earlier this summer."

"Yes, she did! Great. Then everything will be fixed," Izzy said, putting her arm around her brother.

"Well, actually, we have another, even bigger problem," Daniel said. "Green Creek is the water source for much of the town, and lately, people are taking more water from the creek than it can sustain."

"Can't you just ask people to use less water?" Brooke asked.

"Unfortunately, we can't. There's a complex system of water rights in this town, and basically, everyone who's taking water has the right to it. The problem is that people are using more and more and more, and pretty soon we'll be at risk of running out of water."

"Wow. And we thought we could fix everything by just putting Rana and his friends in buckets in Izzy and Zack's garage," Brooke said. "People must really take a lot of showers."

"Don't forget, people use water for all kinds of things," Daniel said. "Cooking, washing, filling swimming pools, and watering lawns."

"My grandma likes to water her lawn," Zack said while trying to shove a stick into his splint.

"That's one of the problems. A lot of people in this town have lawns," Victoria said. "It wouldn't be a problem if we lived in a rainy place like Syracuse, New York. There, the grass grows so quickly that people have to mow their lawns multiple times throughout the summer. But around here, it's so dry that people have to water their lawns every few days. It takes more water than the creek can provide."

"But we love lawns and fields, and we need pastures for our horses," Tai said.

"I get that," Daniel said. "I played soccer growing up and still do—but we need to be smart about it if we don't want to run out of water for ourselves and our aquatic friends."

"My dad used to water our lawn with a big sprinkler in the afternoons. A few years ago, he turned half of the lawn into a native plant garden, which he doesn't have to water at all. I helped. He still waters the lawn half, but only a few days a week and always in the morning. He says in the morning, less water is lost to evaporation than would be lost during the hot part of the day. He doesn't even use a hose; he reuses water from his showers that he catches in a bucket. I didn't really get it until now," Brooke said.

"That's fantastic," Victoria said. "If everyone in

town did that, we'd be in better shape."

"Can we help Grandma Pearl put a native garden in?" Zack asked Izzy.

"I guess. I just don't know anything about it," she answered. "Brooke, could you show us how?"

"Yes! I learned a lot when dad put in ours," Brooke offered.

"I'll help, too," Tai said.

"It sounds like you kids have your work cut out for you," Victoria said. "And speaking of the Nature Club, how is the fundraising going for the swim-a-thon?"

"We had enough sponsors to raise the money with all four of us swimming," Izzy said slowly.

Tai lifted one eyebrow. "But now only three of us will be swimming."

Zack looked down at his dirty feet. "It will be my fault if we don't raise enough money for the fence," he said quietly.

"Your fault?" Tai asked. "No way. Nobody asks for a broken arm. If we don't make enough to fix the whole fence, we'll just use what we do get on a year's worth of ice cream sundaes!"

Zack, however, wasn't laughing. But he also wasn't crying—he was focused on shoving a stick down into his splint to scratch his itch.

9

When the kids left the creek, they went straight to Brooke's house to ask her dad for help. He taught graphic design at the local college during the school year and was off during the summer, allowing him to spend time with the kids. It seemed like they always had some new project idea, and his design skills often came in handy.

"We need your help," Brooke told her dad as soon as she and her friends burst through the door. "We need to fix Izzy and Zack's grandma's lawn, paint the drains, and teach everyone about the watershed.

"Whoa," Mr. Clark said. "That's a lot—even for you kids."

"But Dad," Brooke said, "we have to protect Green Creek."

"And if we don't, Rana could die," Zack said.

Mr. Clark looked down at Zack, who hardly talked to adults, and nodded. "Preserving Green Creek to protect the life that depends on it is very important. I'm happy to help," Mr. Clark said.

"Thanks, Dad!" Brooke said, while the others nodded and smiled.

"Now . . . you will be more successful if you map out a plan. Are you really planning to do all of those things? Let's see, what were they? The lawn, the drains, the education, and was there anything else?" Mr. Clark asked.

The kids all nodded.

"And this is all *in addition* to the swim-a-thon?" Mr. Clark asked.

"Yup," Tai answered. "These projects will protect the water in the creek. The swim-a-thon will raise money to fix the fence that protects the meadow next to the creek."

"Except . . . ," Zack said looking down. "Except the swim-a-thon is now ruined because I broke my stupid arm."

"Your arm isn't stupid—but using that ladder

wasn't exactly smart," Izzy said.

"Okay now," Mr. Clark interjected. "We all make mistakes and Zack clearly feels badly about it. Anyway, isn't there someone else who can swim for him?"

"But we're all there is, Dad," Brooke said. "You are looking at the entire Nature Club."

"I thought there was another member. When I made your T-shirts, I remember making a fifth one and mailing it to someone. Who was that?"

"Do you mean Miguel?" Izzy suggested.

"Yes, that's it. Miguel. Why don't you ask him to do Zack's laps?

"Dad! Miguel is Izzy's pen pal. He lives in Nicaragua," Brooke said. "He can't do it."

"Maybe he can," Zack said, perking up. "Izzy, you said he lives near a lake."

"Wait a minute, Zack. Are you asking if Miguel can do the swim-a-thon from Nicaragua?" Brooke said, her eyes wide with enthusiasm.

"Why not?!" Izzy exclaimed. "Miguel told me he loves to swim."

63

"I like it!" Tai said.

"Then we wouldn't just have Green County's first swim-a-thon, we'd have Green County's first *international* swim-a-thon!" Brooke exclaimed.

"Izzy, can you ask him? Please?" Zack pleaded.

"You are welcome to use my phone to call him—but please use one of those free apps. It's international, after all," Mr. Clark offered.

"Thanks Mr. Clark, but we . . . ," Izzy paused.

"They only write because they are pen pals." Brooke finished for her. "They don't even like using email—they mail letters."

"Except we do use email when we're in a rush . . . like now," Izzy said quickly.

"Well then, you are welcome to use my computer," Mr. Clark offered.

"Thanks, Dad!" Brooke said and ran to the room where her dad had his computer with her friends following.

Brooke got the computer started and opened up the email but pushed the computer toward Izzy. "He's your pen pal; you should write it."

"Oh. Okay," Izzy said. She typed in his email address and began writing:

Dear Miguel,

"Dear Miguel?" Tai interrupted. "That is one serious email."

"Really, Izzy, is that how you write emails?" Brooke added. "You sound like my grandma."

"Jeez. Maybe I should go write in a room by myself," Izzy said defensively.

"No way—I want to be there," Zack said. "All this is happening because of me."

"Okay, I'll stay, but you guys need to stop picking on me."

Starting again, Izzy wrote:

Dear Miguel,

Izzy looked at Tai and Brooke, and when they didn't interrupt this time, she continued,

The Nature Club signed up for a swim-a-thon. We are raising money to repair a fence that protects a meadow at Green County Park. The way it works is that all four of us—Tai, Brooke, Zack, and I—swim for an hour. Then we add our laps together and get paid by the sponsors based on the total number of laps. The problem is, Zack broke his arm—

This time, Zack interrupted. "Make sure to tell him I am getting an orange cast."

Izzy looked at Zack and rolled her eyes and then continued:

and is getting an orange cast. That also means he can't swim.

Anyway, we got this idea that maybe you could swim at the same time and we could count your laps. That way, we'd still have four swimmers—

"And," Brooke interrupted. "We'd have an international swim-a-thon."

Izzy took a deep breath and continued typing:

and we'd have an international swim-a-thon. We looked up the time difference and Nicaragua is two hours ahead of California. So if you swim, you would swim at noon when we swim at 10am.

Will you do it? We really need you.

"Can you say please?" Zack asked.

Izzy deleted the last two sentences and typed:

Will you please do it? We really need you, and it would mean the world to Zack.

Your friend,
Izzy

"Perfect!" Brooke said.

"Well done," Tai added.

"Thanks, Izzy," Zack whispered.

Knowing Miguel only checked his email at

night, they didn't wait for a response. Instead, they returned to Mr. Clark and sketched out a plan for accomplishing all they wanted to do to protect the creek.

10

The next day, the kids got started on their plan. They would contact all the people who needed to give them permission, then get supplies, and finally, get started on the actual work.

Mr. Clark helped Brooke call Janet Helling from the county to get a map of all the storm drains in town. The Nature Club had worked with Janet earlier that summer to protect milkweed habitat for monarchs, so she was happy to hear from them. Brooke talked, but she put the phone on speaker so her dad could listen.

"Hi, Brooke, how are you and your friends?" Janet asked.

"We're doing great, but we are worried about Green Creek. People are dumping oil into the storm drains, and it's getting into the creek."

"Oh, I agree with you. And it isn't just oil—it's

oil and paint and all kinds of chemicals."

"The poor animals!" Brooke cried.

"The poor everything alive," Janet agreed. "Something really needs to change."

"We have an idea. We want to paint signs on the curbs next to the drains to teach people they go straight to Green Creek. Victoria Perez said we should call you to get permission to do it," Brooke explained.

"That would be terrific," Janet responded. "I've wanted to paint signs on those drains for years— I've already got it approved, but I've never had time to design a stencil and then paint them. I even already have the paint."

"It isn't purple by any chance?" Brooke asked.

"Purple? No," Janet laughed. "It's dark blue to make people think of water."

Brooke looked at her dad and made a face. He looked at his daughter, who was wearing purple from head to toe, and held his hand over his mouth so as not to laugh out loud.

"O-kaaay . . . ," Brooke said slowly, "I guess

blue will work."

"I'm thrilled you kids want to take on this project," Janet said. "With your help, I bet we could get it done in half a day." They talked a bit about what the logo should say and then made a plan to meet the next morning to do the actual painting.

Meanwhile, Izzy and Zack were making their way to Grandma Pearl's house. They stopped by their own house to check in with their mom and found her in the back yard, near the old willow tree and the still-broken ladder. "Hi, Mom," Izzy said. "We are going to Grandma Pearl's to change her lawn into a native plant garden so she uses less water."

"To save the frogs," Zack added.

"That sounds terrific. Then maybe you can help me. I'm looking for a good spot to put in an herb garden and I really know nothing about gardening." Then she added, "Do you know what you're doing?"

"No, but Brooke does," Zack answered. Then

he ran off to catch up with Izzy, who was already making her way to Grandma Pearl's.

When they arrived, Grandma Pearl was out in the yard, reading in her hammock. "What adventure are you having today?" she asked over her book.

"We want to change your garden to help the frogs," Zack said.

"Don't worry, all my garden fairies and gnomes are watching over all the frogs," Grandma Pearl said, gesturing to her array of metal sculptures.

"Grandma, we want to know if we can change your lawn into a native plant garden," Izzy said. "Then you won't have to water it as much, and there would be more water in Green Creek."

"For the frogs," Zack added.

Grandma Pearl put down her book and sat up. "That is a terrific idea." She suggested they pick plants used by butterflies and other pollinators to make the garden even more beneficial. They took measurements, made a list of supplies they would need, and planned to do the work the next afternoon.

Tai was also busy making arrangements. Since he had a bike, he rode over to Green County Garden Supply to talk to the owner about creating a display about native plants and hanging a sign about water conservation.

"Great idea," said one of the employees who overheard their conversation said. "Our state is drying up."

The owner nodded and said, "You know what Tai? We aren't just going to let you hang up your sign. We are going to create a display of native plants to put with your sign." She then turned to the employee and said, "Hey, Grace, how about we spend the rest of the day doing that so it's ready when he comes back with his sign tomorrow?"

"Terrific," Grace responded. "I can also make Tai a list of things to include on his sign."

By the time Tai pedaled off, Grace had given him a list and the owner was already busy creating a display.

Tai's next stop was Green County Oil and Lube. There, he asked the owners if they'd be willing to hang a sign about how to recycle used motor oil. "You are speaking my language," the owner said. "It makes me crazy when customers don't recycle their oil. An absolute 'yes' is your answer." He made a list of what should be on the sign and gave it to Tai.

As planned, the kids reconvened that afternoon and shared their successes. They decided they would gather all the supplies they needed and then spend the afternoon making the stencils and signs and planning the garden.

Mr. Clark had everything they needed, so they got started right away. They created a design for the storm drains, and Mr. Clark converted it into a stencil. It said, "Protect Green Creek—Only Rain in the Drain" with a picture of a frog. Then they made signs for proper paint and oil disposal for the hardware store and gas station.

As they worked, Zack kept shoving paint brushes into his splint to itch his arm. "Too bad you didn't get a removable one," Mr. Clark said. "You do realize you could cause yourself an infection, right?"

When they were done, Mr. Clark took them to drop off the signs and then made them all dinner. They made a plan to meet the next morning to paint the drains with Janet Helling. Then, while Zack got his cast in the afternoon, the others would work on Grandma Pearl's garden. If they had time, they would also get in a swim practice.

11

Rana now had a fully developed mouth and a functioning digestive system. His tail had shrunken down so much that it was barely visible. His transformation was almost complete.

Rana swam to the surface and climbed onto a floating log. He breathed in deeply. He tested out his legs. His right leg was stronger, but he was now able to use both. Then he jumped to shore. There, he landed in the thick grass at the edge of the meadow.

He traveled slowly, favoring his right leg, moving through the tall blades of grass. He became aware of a line of tiny ants traveling across a boulder at the edge of the meadow. He moved toward them and then crawled up on the boulder, relying on the sticky pads on his toes. He grabbed a few ants with his muscular tongue.

It was good to eat, but after days of hardly eating, he needed something more substantial. He spotted a fly sitting high on a nearby plant and sat still to watch it. He lifted up on his back legs to jump, but then sat back down—his left leg wasn't strong enough to jump fast enough to catch it.

Instead, he shot out his long tongue and caught the fly in his sticky saliva. In a flash, he snapped his tongue back into his mouth and closed his eyes while he gulped it down.

12

The next day, the kids met Janet as planned and got right to work. The painting went quickly, and they were done before lunch. After having lunch together, Zack headed home while the others headed off to Grandma Pearl's house.

When Zack walked in, he found his mother in the kitchen, grimacing as she sipped her coffee.

"I know it's better for me to drink coffee without sugar, but I just can't get used to this taste," she said. Then, looking at Zack's filthy, paint-splattered splint, she added, "Are you ready for that cast?"

"At least it will be orange," Zack said. He was so itchy he was actually starting to be excited about the cast.

"Yes, at least it will be orange," his mother agreed with a smile. "And now, with Miguel swimming, you don't have to worry about raising enough money anymore."

"But Mom, he hasn't been practicing; what if he can't swim enough laps?"

"Hmm," his mother thought for a moment. "We don't have to leave for another hour. Maybe you can get another pledge from someone to take some pressure off the others for swimming enough laps. Why don't you run next door and ask Mr. Farooq to sponsor the team? He wasn't home when you asked around before."

"Will you go with me?" Zack asked. He had only asked for pledges with the others and didn't want to ask for one by himself. He wasn't shy, exactly, he just wasn't comfortable talking to adults he didn't know.

"You can do it. I'll watch you from the porch," Mrs. Philips responded.

Zack grunted and walked out the front door. When he got to Mr. Farooq's house, he very slowly lifted his finger to the doorbell and rang it.

Nothing happened.

He rang it again.

Suddenly, the door swung open and Mr. Farooq stood there smiling. "Zack! How are you, and how is your arm? Your mother told me you had broken it."

"Fine."

"What color cast are you getting this afternoon?"

"Orange."

"Orange, huh? Good choice."

Zack just stared at him and nodded.

"Is there something I can help you with today?" Mr. Farooq asked.

"We need more pledges for the swim-a-thon."

"It doesn't look like you'll get many laps done with that arm."

Again, Zack just stared.

"Am I right?" Mr. Farooq asked.

"Miguel will swim for me," he replied quietly.

Mr. Farooq didn't know who Miguel was, but rather than ask more questions, he knew how to get Zack interested. "Want to see my pet turtle?"

"Yes."

Mr. Farooq walked across the room to a large tank, took out a turtle, and brought it back to show Zack. It was a pretty yellow-and-green patterned turtle with bright-red marks over the ears. "She's a red-eared slider. I got her on a trip to San Francisco. Isn't she pretty?"

Zack nodded.

"I've had her for many years, but now I need to release her. I'm too old to keep her tank clean. I've been trying to think of where to put her and I've decided she would like Green Creek—especially with all the great work your Nature Club is doing to keep it clean.

"What do you think about releasing her there for me? That's something you can do with one arm. How about you do that for me, and then I'll set you up with a pledge for your swim-a-thon?"

Zack nodded.

"Okay, then. I'll put her in a bucket and after you've dropped her off, bring my bucket back to me and I'll give you a pledge."

Again, Zack nodded.

Mr. Farooq wandered off into the house and came back with a cardboard box. He put his turtle in the box and then the box in a bucket and handed it to Zack.

Zack ran back to his house. His mom, who had watched the whole interaction from her porch, shook her head at Zack when he arrived. "Please tell me you aren't coming home with a new pet."

"Nope. Mr. Farooq said after I release his turtle into the creek, he will give us a pledge."

"Okay. If we leave now, we can do it on the way to get your cast."

When they got to the creek, Daniel was there. "Hello there, Zack. What have you got in the bucket?"

"My neighbor's turtle. He asked me to release it for him."

"What?" Daniel said, eyes wide. "You can't release pets here." Then he peered into the bucket. "Oh no, definitely not. It's a red-eared slider. Those are the worst."

"The worst?" Zack repeated. "I think it's amazing."

Daniel laughed. "I don't mean the turtle is bad. The turtle itself is fine—in its own habitat. What I mean is, releasing non-native animals is bad, and releasing invasive ones like red-eared sliders is the worst."

"I thought you said animals should be in the wild and not in captivity," Zack said.

"Animals are adapted to live in the places where they evolved. They know how to hide from predators there, they know how to find food there, and they know how to find shelter there. When you move them to new places, they tend to either suffer or cause problems.

"On the one hand, they may not be able to find food or the right habitat, or they may be eaten by the native wildlife. On the other hand, they may take up too much of the habitat, bring diseases the native animals can't handle, or even eat the native species.

"An invasive predator like the red-eared slider

is even worse," he continued, "because they reproduce fast and take over quickly. When people buy pets, they need to be willing to care for them throughout their entire lives. Turtles live a long time, so people get tired of caring for them and then release them. Another problem animal that people often release is bullfrogs. They are gobbling up all kinds of native species, including the little chorus frogs."

"But I love bullfrogs," Zack said. "They are all over my aunt's house in Pennsylvania."

"Bullfrogs are native to Pennsylvania, so they aren't a problem there," Daniel said.

"Oh . . . ," Zack said, thinking through what Daniel just said.

Zack's mom beeped the car horn and yelled from the car where she was waiting, "Zack, please hurry or we'll be late."

"I'll tell you what," Daniel said. "I'll take the turtle and find it a good owner while you go and get that cast."

"Thanks," Zack said, handing Daniel the box

with the turtle. "I'm sorry. I didn't know."

"Don't worry about it! I think most people don't know. If your club has any ideas about how to spread the word, let me know."

13

When Zack got home from the hospital, he was wearing a bright-orange cast. Brooke, Izzy, and Tai were all at the house when he got there. With the help of Grandma Pearl and Mr. Clark, they had done all they could to get started converting Grandma Pearl's lawn to a native plant garden and had even made it to the local pool to practice for the swim-a-thon.

"What an awesome color! Can we sign it?" Brooke asked.

Mrs. Philips handed Brooke a black marker.

Brooke drew a line of bear tracks that appeared to be walking across Zack's cast and then signed her name. Izzy wrote her name followed by, "Nature Club forever!" Tai drew a cowboy riding a horse.

"Cool!" Zack remarked, examining the

signatures.

"It looks like you had a good day after all," Izzy said with a smile.

"I like the orange and I like not itching anymore . . . but I didn't end up getting a pledge from Mr. Farooq."

"What pledge?" Izzy asked.

"I tried to get a pledge from Mr. Farooq for the swim-a-thon. He said if I released his turtle into Green Creek, he'd give me a pledge."

"Mr. Farooq had a pet turtle? That's so cool," Brooke said.

"Did the turtle like the creek?" Brooke asked.

"That's the problem. I never released it because I saw Daniel at the creek and he stopped me from doing it."

"Why'd he do that?"

"He said that animals shouldn't be moved from one environment into another because they can get eaten, eat others, mess up the habitat, or spread disease. He said the turtle I was going to release—a red-eared slider—is one of the worst."

"Ohhh . . . ," Izzy said. "I guess we should know that. What did you do with it?"

"I had to get to the hospital, so Daniel said he'd find it a good home and took it."

"Why did Mr. Farooq want to get rid of his turtle?" Brooke asked.

"He said it was too hard to clean his tank," Zack said.

"What if we clean his tank for him?" Brooke suggested.

"It's a little late now," Izzy pointed out.

"What did he do with the tank?" Tai asked. "I bet the new owner will need it."

"It was still in the living room when I left—and it was really dirty," Zack said.

"Maybe if we clean it for him, he'll still sponsor us," Tai said.

"Maybe he'll still sponsor us, anyway," Brooke said. "You did get rid of the turtle for him—just not into the creek."

"Do we still need another sponsor? How'd you do on laps at practice?" Zack asked.

"We're a little short. I can't swim very fast without my goggles," Izzy said. "It would be great if Mr. Farooq could sponsor us—just in case."

The kids looked at each other. "It's worth a try," Brooke said.

They went next door and knocked. Mr. Farooq answered quickly and smiled. "Zack, you're back—and with your friends. How did my turtle do in the creek?"

"Um . . . I . . . Um . . . ," Zack said.

"Did you release her?" Mr. Farooq asked.

"He couldn't," Izzy answered for Zack. "He ran into Daniel, who studies frogs, and he said not to release non-native animals. He said since they aren't used to the area, they often die but sometimes they live and make things hard on the native animals."

"Because they eat them," Zack added.

"Right. They eat up the native animals!" Brooke said.

"Oh no. I didn't even think about that. So what did you do with her?" Mr. Farooq asked.

"Daniel took her to find her a new home," Zack explained.

"Well, then, someone will need my tank. But it's a mess."

"We thought we'd clean it for you," Tai said, looking at the others for acknowledgement.

"Well, isn't that nice. I will gladly take you up on that offer. And I haven't forgotten about your swim-a-thon. You took care of my turtle problem—even if it was in a different way than I'd imagined—so I will give you a pledge."

Zack let out a big sigh. "Thank you," he said.

The kids took the tank outside and scrubbed it. Then they loaded it into the back of Mrs. Philips's truck so she could drop it off at the county office.

"Now we might actually raise enough money," Izzy said. "I just wish I had my goggles to really give it my best. I can swim so much better when I can see and my eyes don't hurt."

"I think I learned something," Zack said hesitantly. "I think I learned it's important to take care of our environment. I'm going to clean my room and look for your goggles."

"What? Really? You're volunteering to pick up your room?" Brooke said, knowing Zack would do anything to avoid picking up.

"That is great news Zack. I'll help you," Izzy offered.

"Maybe we should all spend a little time on cleanup today," Tai said. "At my place, the back shed is a mess."

"Good idea," Brooke said. "I don't even think we cleaned up all my dad's art supplies yesterday."

The kids all went home to spend some time picking up. When Izzy and Zack got to their house, they found their mom and Cody in the kitchen. They said a quick "hi" and went straight to Zack's room.

His room was so messy it didn't take long to make progress. They quickly found some missing library books, Zack's long-lost baseball glove, an old sandwich, and finally . . . Izzy's goggles under a heap of dirty clothes.

"Hooray!" Izzy yelled.

Mrs. Philips, curious about what they were doing and hearing the shouts of celebration, came up to check on them. Cody followed her. "I can't believe it," Mrs. Philips said. "It looks amazing in here. I'll join you in picking up—I'll work on the kitchen."

"And while you are doing that, I'll go outside and fix that ladder," Cody said.

"Great. How about if we all work hard for thirty minutes and then come back together for a drink," Mrs. Philips said as she set a timer.

"But Mom, we already started," Zack said.

"And just imagine how great your room will look after another thirty minutes!" she responded.

In half an hour, after first admiring their work, they all met in the kitchen for a celebratory drink. Izzy and Zack had lemonade, and Mrs. Philips and Cody had coffee—with sugar. "You know, that didn't even take long," Mrs. Philips said. "I think I've spent more time this summer looking for things I've lost than I just spent picking up."

Just then, the doorbell rang. It was Brooke.

"Hi, Mrs. Philips. Hi Izzy and Zack," Brooke said. "Did Miguel write back?"

"I don't know, but let's find out," Izzy said. Brooke and Zack followed Izzy back to Mrs. Philips's computer and peered over her shoulder as she checked.

"He did!" Izzy said. "It says, 'Dear Izzy,'"

"Wow, he also writes his emails formally," Brooke interrupted.

Izzy growled and rolled her eyes. "Do you want me to read it or not?"

"Read it!" Brooke smiled and made a gesture as if she were zipping her lips closed.

Izzy continued, "Of course I can swim. I live right near a beautiful lake. My brothers will help me measure off the distance to equal a lap in your pool and will time me. My brother will message your dad the number of laps right when I finish. This will be a lot of fun! Saludos, Miguel."

"Awesome!" Brooke yelled. Brooke and Izzy high-fived each other.

"I don't get it," Zack whispered to Izzy.

"Don't get what?" Izzy asked.

"Why he has to swim earlier—or is it later?" Zack said.

"Time zones are confusing," Izzy said. "The Earth is divided into twenty-four time zones because there are twenty-four hours in a day. Nicaragua falls into a different zone than California. It's all based on the position of the sun in the sky. In other words, times are different, so everyone gets noon when the sun is high in the sky."

"Speaking of time . . . you kids better get some rest tonight if you want to be at your best tomorrow," Mrs. Philips said.

"Except me," Zack said. "I can stay up all night since I'm not swimming."

"You are the cheering section, and that is a critical job," Mrs. Philips said.

"Yeah, right," Zack said downcast. "They won't

even hear me from the water."

"Zack, we will know you're there, and that matters a lot," Izzy said.

"Seriously, Zack," Brooke added, "we need you there as part of the team."

"Okay," Mrs. Philips said, "time for all of you to get some rest."

Brooke went home, and Izzy and Zack got ready for bed. That night, Izzy quickly fell asleep, but not Zack. He tossed and turned and listened to the night sounds through the open window.

14

Now that Rana could easily breathe through both his nose and mouth, he was able to spend most of his time in the meadow. He was well camouflaged, so he didn't have to stay hidden all the time to be safe, but during the heat of the day, he spent most of his time in the shade. Like all frogs, he had a waxy coating that helped him stay moist, but he still had to be careful to avoid drying out. He also now slept a lot during the day and was most active in the evening.

As the sun set, the air cooled down. Rana moved out into the open at the edge of the creek. He took a few deep breaths and let the air back out through his mouth. Then he took another deep breath, but this time, he kept his mouth and nose shut, making his throat bulge out. When the air flowed over his vocal chords, it made a call that sounded like, "kre-r-r-ek." Although Rana was less than two inches long, the sound could be heard way into the distance.

A raccoon, attracted to his call, patrolled the edge of the river, looking for him. A frog would be a tasty snack. Rana heard the raccoon's approach and quickly slipped back into the clean, clear water.

15

The next morning, although Zack got little sleep, he ran downstairs at first light.

"Mom, I don't have a lot of time, and I have a lot to do!" he said.

Mrs. Philips was just pouring her first cup of coffee. "What?" Mrs. Philips asked. "Why are you even awake?"

"I have to get my display ready," he explained. "Last night, when I couldn't sleep, I heard Rana talking to me. He told me to make a display."

"Rana was talking to you, huh?" Izzy said as she stumbled down the stairs.

"Well, maybe not talking to me . . . but talking," Zack said. "When I was lying in bed listening to the frogs in the distance, I knew what my job would be today. I'm going to teach people about native animals so they don't release their non-native pets into Rana's habitat."

"That's a great idea," Izzy said. "I'll help you."

Before Mrs. Philips could even add sugar to her coffee, they were pulling out cardboard, markers, scissors, and tape to get started. "I guess I'll make pancakes while you creative geniuses do your thing," she said.

"Thanks, Mom," Izzy said. "It sounds like me and Zack will both need our energy today!"

When they were done and had eaten their fill of pancakes, Izzy checked her email. There was a message from Miguel. He wrote that his brother had used buoys—anchored orange floats—to mark off the distance he would swim back and forth in the lake. He was ready to swim.

"This is amazing!" Izzy said. "Come on Zack, let's go meet the others." Izzy grabbed her goggles from the shelf by the door where she decided she would now carefully store them, and they ran out of the house.

In minutes, Izzy and Zack were with Brooke and Tai at the pool. They were all wearing the matching Nature Club T-shirts Mr. Clark had made them earlier that summer. Izzy and Zack excitedly explained Zack's display to the others. Then Zack set it up while the others stretched and looked around.

There were five teams in total, each raising money for a different cause ranging from the community food bank to meal deliveries for the elderly. It was exciting to see so many people from the community either swimming or coming to watch, all with the goal of helping others.

Zack had envisioned being miserable all day, but instead, not only was he caught up in the excitement, but he was busy. Before he was done setting up, several people had already stopped by his table to learn about native species.

Then, at 9:50, all the teams were called to the pool, and right at ten a.m., the starting buzzer went off. As the kids swam, Zack cheered. He no longer cared if they could hear him or not—he was just excited to be part of the event.

When the hour was up and the laps were

counted, the Nature Club couldn't believe it—they had swum ten more laps than expected—mostly due to Izzy, who credited it to having her goggles. Then Miguel's brother sent over a message with his laps. Not only had he done what they'd hoped, but he had also completed an additional seven. In the end, they were going to bring in an extra seven hundred twenty-five dollars in pledge money.

As they celebrated, Zack noticed one of the other groups wasn't quite as happy. It was the group swimming for the local food bank. Although they had done their best, they had come in a little short of their goal.

"Can we give them our extra?" Zack asked.

"Yes!" the others answered in unison.

"Thanks for being adaptable," Zack said, and they all laughed.

Then Izzy held up her water bottle. "I think it's time for a toast."

The other kids joined her.

"To protecting our watershed!" Izzy said.

"And to helping others!" Brooke exclaimed.

"And to being adaptable!" Tai added while nudging Zack.

"And to frogs!" Zack said.

That afternoon, the kids stayed around the pool. All the groups were feeling excited about their accomplishments and ready to just have fun diving and splashing around. It was late when they finally left. The Nature Club kids and their families all went over the Philipses' house for a barbecue where the house was clean and the food was already laid out.

"Wow," Mrs. Clark said to Mrs. Philips, "your house looks amazing."

"Thank you, Nicole," Scarlet responded. "I doubt it will always look this good, but at least at won't look as bad as it did."

Mrs. Clark laughed. "Don't worry, when it does, I'll come over to help you—I still owe you some help—as I promised."

The group ate on blankets in the yard. At some point in the meal, every single one of them even got to watch a woodpecker carry grubs to the hole in the old willow tree.

Then, finally, it started getting dark and it was time to clean up. Everyone pitched in and then met around an outdoor fire to roast marshmallows. It had been such a great day that they kept reliving it over and over.

"I wish Miguel was here with us," Izzy said.

"I wish Rana was here with us," Zack said.

"I bet if he was, he'd give you a big 'thank-you'," Izzy said.

They sat quietly for a bit, listening to the sound of the crickets set against the otherwise silent night. Then in the distance came the unmistakable sound of a chorus frog. *Kre-eeeck*.

"I suppose he just did," Zack laughed. The day was complete.

Notes on Pacific Chorus Frogs

by Zack Philips

Pacific chorus frogs, also known as *Pseudacris regilla* in Latin, can be green, tan, reddish, or brown and can even change colors! You can identify them by a dark eye stripe that starts near their shoulder, goes across their eye, and ends down at their nose. They also have long, slightly-webbed toes. The adults are really cute. They are less than two inches long. Their calls sound like "ribbit" or "kre-eeck."

Pacific chorus frogs are found at a bunch of different elevations in the western United States. They use ponds, streams, and lakes and are mostly nocturnal. The females lay clumps of up to one hundred eggs in shallow, calm water. They tuck them under leaf litter or other vegetation.

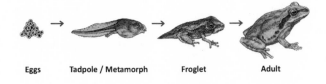

Eggs   Tadpole / Metamorph   Froglet   Adult

The tadpoles feed on algae and pollen. When they transform from tadpoles to frogs, they also transform from herbivores to carnivores—but it's not what we think of when we think of carnivores. For them, carnivore means eating insects and spiders.

✳✳✳

Here's what people can do to protect frogs and other amphibians and reptiles:

- Protect natural water flow and quality and native habitats.

- Never release pets into the wild. They can spread disease and eat native wildlife.

- Reduce, reuse, recycle, and pick up litter to protect their habitats and keep wildlife from choking on trash.

- Keep cats indoors and dogs on leashes so they don't disturb or eat the frogs.

- Have a chemical-free garden to not poison any frogs, their habitats, or their prey.

Questions to Consider:

1. Zack breaks his arm when he falls out of a tree. Have you ever broken a bone?

2. Zack can't swim in the swim-a-thon because of his broken arm. How did he react to that news? How would you react?

3. What are the potential challenges the tadpoles, frogs, and metamorphs face?

4. How does Zack end up contributing to the swim-a-thon effort?

5. How did businesses around town contribute to the swim-a-thon effort?

6. Water conservation is important in maintaining the habitat at Green Creek. What are ways to conserve water in your home?

7. Do you know where your water comes from?

Join the Nature Club
for more adventures!

www.natureclubbooks.com

Read on for a peek at Book 5 . . .

We All Are One
Chapter 1

"Next stop, Greenley Station. *Fiiiiive* minutes," the conductor announced as he hurried through the train. "Please gather near the doors. It will be a short stop."

"That's our stop," Miguel said to his mother, who was eyeing him questioningly.

"*Estamos allá,*" she translated while poking her husband in the row ahead of them. Miguel's dad was the only one in the family who didn't speak any English, with the exception of a few words for greetings and directions. He nodded and stood up to lower their bags from the overhead racks.

"*Permítame ayudarte Papá,*" said Miguel, jumping up to help his father. Together, they lowered their three suitcases while Miguel's mother gathered the waste from their café car lunch of pizza, soft pretzels, and soda.

"So much waste," she said, shaking her head. "Where should I put it?"

"There's a garbage down near the bathroom. I'll take it," Miguel said, grabbing the pile of trash from her and then making his way down the aisle. He threw the non-recyclable trash into the garbage but tossed the empty bottles into the blue bin next to it. "At least part of our lunch isn't going into a landfill," he said to himself.

Miguel then rejoined his parents to grab his soccer ball and suitcase and help them stumble down the aisle with their luggage while the train rattled along.

"Now arriving at Greenley Station," the conductor's voice crackled over the speaker. The train's bells rang loudly until, finally, the train screeched into the station. As it lurched to a halt, Miguel's mother fell against him.

"Aye! Mamá, are you okay?" he asked.

"Oh yes, except . . . ," she stopped, realizing she had knocked her glasses off. Quickly shoving them back onto her head, she put them on upside down, sending Miguel into a fit of laughter.

"What, you don't like them like this?" asked

his mother, joining him in laughter until they both had tears in their eyes. Although Señor Ramirez looked at them crossly, Miguel was grateful for the laugh. It gave him some relief from the edginess he'd felt all day. It had been many hours of travel by plane and then train to get from his home in Nicaragua to Izzy's town in Northern California.

His parents had been invited to attend a meeting of organic coffee growers in San Francisco. As a leader in converting conventional coffee farms to organic, his mother was even asked to give the closing speech at the Friday night banquet.

Although Señor and Señora Ramirez had five children, Miguel was their youngest and the only one who still lived with them. Since Miguel had a pen pal, Izzy Philips, who lived in California, his parents had decided to bring him on the trip so he could visit her in person.

Izzy's mom, Mrs. Philips, had offered to pick Miguel up in San Francisco, but Señora Ramirez insisted on delivering him herself. After all, it was Miguel's first time outside of Nicaragua *and* his first time away from his parents for a whole week.

As Miguel stepped off the train, his stomach felt tight and queasy. He took a deep breath, telling himself it was just nerves, and then helped his parents down from the train and onto the platform.

"*Espero que ellos no te olviden*," his father worried, looking around.

"*No se preocupe, Papá*," said Miguel. "Izzy will not forget me." Just as he said that, a girl with straight, brown hair pulled back into a ponytail pulling a younger boy with bright-red hair by the hand ran up to them, asking, "Are you Miguel?"

"Izzy!" Miguel responded, smiling broadly.

"I'm so glad you're here," Izzy said and gave him an awkward hug.

"Me too!" he responded. Miguel then put his arm warmly around the boy, saying, "And you must be Zack."

"How did you know?" Zack asked.

"By your penguin," Miguel said, nodding toward the large stuffed penguin Zack was holding tightly in his right arm. "Izzy says Otto is always with you."

"Oh," Zack said, smiling.

"And by your *enyesado*," Miguel said, nodding toward the orange cast on Zack's left arm.

"You have a great memory," Izzy said with a laugh. She then straightened and looked at Miguel's parents. "Hi. I mean, um, *bienvenidos Señor y Señora Ramírez*," she mumbled self-consciously.

Before they could answer, Mrs. Philips walked up carrying Izzy's littlest brother, Carson, in her arms. "Welcome!" she said, holding out her hand to Señor Ramirez and giving Señora Ramirez a warm hug. "We are so happy to finally meet you. Izzy so values her friendship with Miguel and is thrilled to spend a week with him."

"Thank you. Miguel feels the same about Izzy, and I am so happy to meet you, too," Señora Ramirez said while her husband watched awkwardly. Miguel and Izzy's teachers had set them up as pen pals more than two years earlier, so Izzy could practice writing in Spanish and Miguel could practice writing in English while they learned about each other's cultures. While most kids in their classes had stopped writing to their pen pals long ago, Miguel and Izzy had kept writing and had formed a strong friendship.

Turning to Señor Ramirez, Mrs. Philips asked, "How is your . . . um, I mean, well, do you speak any English?"

"*Un poco*," he answered. "*Muy poco.*"

"And I don't speak a word of Spanish," Mrs. Philips said apologetically.

"Don't worry about him," Miguel's mom said. "I'll translate for him. Or we can just ignore him." She laughed while Señor Ramirez rolled his eyes, knowing her well enough to assume the joke was on him.

"I'll let that be *your* call," Mrs. Philips said, smiling. "Now, for planning purposes, what time is your train back to San Francisco?"

"It leaves at seven o'clock," Miguel's mom replied. "We already have tickets."

"Oh no, that only gives us an hour. I was hoping to make you a nice meal at our house, but given the limited time, let's just grab a quick meal at the station café.

"That sounds fine," Miguel's mom said. "Although we only need something to drink," she added, patting her stomach. "We ate the entire way here."

The two families wandered over to the café and enjoyed a drink together. While the others had lemonade served in frosted glass mugs, Miguel ordered a bottle of cold soda. He hoped the bubbles would settle his gurgling stomach.

Then it was time for Señor and Señora Ramirez to head back to the city. The Philipses wished them a good trip and they exchanged contact information. They waited at the café while Miguel tossed his bottle into the recycling bin before helping his parents onto their train.

"*Sé bueno y escucha a la Señora Philips,*" Señor

Ramirez said, handing Miguel some money for the week and giving him a big hug.

"*Por supuesto, Papa, no se preocupe. Lo amo,*" Miguel replied. Then he turned to his mother. "Good luck, *Mamá*. I know you will be a great speaker."

"I hope. I hope I can make a *diferencia*. If only the California governor would come! Then I could make a real difference," she said.

"If he is smart, he will come, learn, and make things better," Miguel said.

Señora Ramirez smiled at her son and hugged him tightly. "*Te amo, Mijo*, I will miss you. Have a great time and please, call us every night! We will see you next Sunday."

"Don't worry, *Mamá*. I will. *Te amo, Mamá.*" The conductor announced that all visitors needed to exit the train. Miguel gave his parents one last hug and then stepped back down onto the platform, where he waved until the train was out of sight.

to be continued . . .

Acknowledgments

I am grateful to Wren Sturdevant, Max Sturdevant, John Sturdevant, Elettra Cudignotto, Rachelle Dyer, Allan Mazur, Polly Mazur, Julie Tribe, Lisa Rhudy, Michael Ross, Jennie Goutet, Chuck Carter, Leslie Paladino, Jessica Santina, and Sarah Hoggatt for their help and encouragement.

I am also grateful to Dr. Molly Stephens, ecologist at the School of Natural Sciences, University of California, Merced, who generously provided expert review.

About the Author

Rachel Mazur, Ph.D., is the author of *Speaking of Bears* (Globe Pequot, 2015), the award-winning picture book *If You Were a Bear* (Sequoia Natural History Association, 2008), and many articles for scientific and trade publications. She is passionate about writing stories to connect kids with nature—and inspiring them to protect it. Rachel lives with her husband and two children in El Portal, California, where she oversees the wildlife program at Yosemite National Park.

To learn more about The Nature Club series, please visit natureclubbooks.com.

To learn more about the art of Elettra Cudignotto, please visit elettracudignotto.com.

To learn more about the art of Rachelle Dyer, please visit rachellepaintings.com.

Made in the USA
Middletown, DE
01 February 2020

84043569R00076